Magical ♡ Rescue Vets

Oona the Unicorn

Melody Lockhart

This edition published in 2021 by Arcturus Publishing Limited
26/27 Bickels Yard, 151–153 Bermondsey Street,
London SE1 3HA

Author: Melody Lockhart
Illustrator: Morgan Huff
Editors: Claire Philip, Joe Harris and Donna Gregory
Designers: Jeni Child and Rosie Bellwood

CH007133NT
Supplier 10, Date 0821, Print run 001

Printed in the UK

Contents

Starfall Forest Map

SOFT HENGE

COTTON-TOP MOUNTAINS

WANDERING WOODS

CRYSTAL CAVES

THE VETS' SURGERY

FLUTTERPUFF OAK

MOONFLOWER MEADOW

RAINBOW RIVER

WATER CLIMBS

MAZE WOOD

GNOME TOWN

WILLOW COTTAGE

HONEYBUNNY WARREN

LOLLIPOP ORCHARD

CHIMNEY TREES

SNOWFLAKE VALLEY

FROZEN LAKE

GRUMPLING GROVE

TO OPAL CITY

Chapter 1

Starfall Forest

Rosie opened her eyes. Then she shut them tight again. For one lovely moment, she had imagined she was back in her beautiful rainbow room. But no. The walls here were covered with disgusting toad wallpaper.

Rosie wobbled off the airbed and opened the curtains. She gasped. Starfall Forest was very pretty in the morning light! "Well," she thought, "perhaps I can put one good thing on my list." From under her pillow she pulled out the piece of paper that she had written on last night, called "Why Moving Has Ruined Everything." She had run out of space!

On the other side of the paper she wrote: "Why Moving Might Not Be So Bad." Under this, she listed the morning view, and the big garden she'd get to play in.

Rosie sighed. It had been the worst start to the summer ever. She had left behind all her friends in Opal City to make a new start in a creaky, old, cobweb-covered cottage in the middle of a forest.

"This will be a dream house by the time we've finished decorating," her mother had said, "Just you wait!"

Rosie didn't *want* to wait—she wanted to be back in her beautiful rainbow room, with her friends, in the bustle of the big city. She didn't say that out loud, though.

Her parents said they needed more space and Dad had always wanted to move back to the village he'd grown up in. They were both super-excited. Rosie thought it was a terrible plan.

In Opal City, their sixth-floor apartment had looked out over the park downtown. She loved watching people running, walking dogs, or rushing to school and work. Here, there were no other houses—or people— anywhere to be seen.

"Dad," she called down the stairs, "can we paint my room like a rainbow again?" The only sounds that came back were muffled thumps. Dad was obviously busy.

Rosie looked out over the vast Starfall Forest. Dark treetops stretched away into the distance. She wished with her whole heart that she was back in Opal City, but she couldn't help being fascinated by the trees, which seemed to twinkle and shimmer in the morning light.

Rosie wondered if her parents would let her explore the forest. It was so close, and it looked so interesting.

Every now and then she saw a tree shake a little and wondered what kind of animals might be living there. In her old life she had been leader of the school's wildlife club. Not her old life, she thought, glumly. Her *real* life.

Just then, something totally extraordinary happened. As Rosie watched, some kind of floating object rose up from the forest, not very far from the house, and hung in the air just above the trees. It was rectangular and it rippled gently in the air. There were shapes on top of it, too. It looked exactly like a magic carpet with people sitting on top ... but surely that was ridiculous!

The next moment, it whooshed away through the trees into the distance, leaving behind it a trail of rainbow light, which hung in the air for just a moment.

Rosie stared. Had she *really* just seen that?

Rosie changed out of her nightshirt as quickly as she could, then hurried down the old wooden staircase two steps at a time. She needed a closer look at that carpet! "Dad, where are my binoculars?" she yelled.

She heard a big crash and the sound of tumbling pans, followed by her father's voice. "I'm not sure, pumpkin, we're a little bit busy down here. Can it wait?"

At the bottom of the stairs, her shirt snagged on something. She looked down to see a big snake's head carved around the stair-post, and her sleeve had caught on its fang. "I am *never*," she thought, "going to get used to this place."

She made her way through the arched doorway into the yellow kitchen. It was a mess of half-emptied boxes and upside-down furniture.

"Morning, honey!" Rosie jumped back as a cardboard box spoke to her. Then her mother popped up out of it, dust in her hair. "Breakfast is on the counter."

Her father appeared, holding a hammer in one hand, and an old phone in the other. "Morning, Rosebud!" he said, looking a bit confused. "What was it you were looking for?"

"Never mind." Rosie called, grabbing a banana and a croissant as she slipped out of the back door.

"Croissants are a plus for the new house!" she thought, biting into the buttery pastry as she looked up at the sky. The rainbow trail had disappeared now, but Rosie knew which direction the flying carpet had gone in. The overgrown tangle behind the cottage couldn't have been more different from their pretty little balcony in the city. Rosie ducked under overhanging branches and around spiky bushes as she fought her way to the back of the yard and the forest, keeping her eyes on the spot where she had last seen the flying carpet.

Rosie tried to push aside a particularly overgrown bush, only to find that it wasn't a bush at all, but an old stone fountain. Pulling away the tangled ivy, Rosie saw that it was covered with carvings of animals— including a large bird with outstretched wings, a scaly dragon, and a laughing mermaid.

Rosie was surprised to see that the bowl of the fountain was filled with a crystal-clear pool of water. She was even more surprised that the bottom of the pool was covered with silver coins. She reached into the water and pulled one out. On one side was a star, and on the other was a fish. She had never seen anything like it before, so she tucked it into her pocket to show her parents later.

Looking around, Rosie could see the tumbled-down fence that marked the end of the yard and the start of Starfall Forest. The flying carpet might be just inside! Rosie dashed forward—but paused when she saw that something else was moving nearby …

She looked, but it was just a collection of weedy plant pots, and a small tree stump. Wait, was it a tree stump?

The tree stump seemed to be moving. No, not just moving—walking! It had dainty little legs, twig-like arms, and a strip of moss above its mouth. Rosie giggled to herself. It had a moss-tache! The tree-stump-creature was tipping the plant pots up one by one, and inspecting the area underneath.

Rosie didn't dare to make a sound. She watched, totally fascinated, as the sweet little creature bustled about. It muttered quietly and scratched its head with a twiggy arm.

"Where can it be?" the tree stump said in a creaky voice. As it spoke, the moss on its face jiggled about wildly. "We'll *never* find the unicorn without it."

Suddenly, there was a loud bang from the house. The tree stump jumped in surprise and dashed through a gap in the fence.

"Did it say 'unicorn'?" Rosie asked herself. She thought for a moment and decided to go back to the house to talk to her parents about all the amazing things she'd seen. Her dad had grown up around here, so perhaps he knew something. A unicorn was even more exciting than a flying carpet—maybe this place was going to be fun, after all.

Rosie had been holding her breath without knowing it, and now let it out in a whoosh of excitement. She couldn't keep this to herself. She had to tell her parents right now about the forest, and the magic carpet and the tree stump, and what she'd heard the tree stump say! Surely they'd help her find it?

"Mama! Dad!" she called loudly as she ran through the open back door, the kitchen, and the living room ... right into a stack of boxes, which crashed noisily to the floor.

"Rosie, slow down!" Her father was halfway up a ladder, doing something fiddly involving wires and a screwdriver. "You can't go racing about like that! You'll break something!"

"Your dad's doing a good enough job of that *without* your help," said her mother, giving Rosie a wink. "But hopefully we'll have the electricity back on again soon."

"Dad, Dad, I need to tell you something really exciting!" Rosie began.

"Sorry, pumpkin," he said, "but I really need to concentrate."

"Mama, you're not going to believe wh ... "

A box started vibrating, and Rosie's mother started rummaging in it.

"So that's where my phone got to!" she said, eventually pulling it from the box. "It's the plumber, sweetheart. I want to see if she can come out today." She answered the call and disappeared into the kitchen.

Rosie sighed with frustration. She was fizzing with excitement! Had the tree-stump-creature really said "unicorn"? Well, if her parents were too busy to listen, she'd just have to investigate by herself. She'd tell them about it later.

Back outside, she followed an overgrown path until she found a metal gate. Its catch was rusty, and as it creaked open, she found herself face-to-face with another toad. This one was part of the wrought-iron frame.

From here, a rough sort of path led into the forest, with high grass on either side that tickled her legs. Here and there were bright pink and orange flowers. She'd never seen— or smelled—anything quite like them before.

"Where did you get to, Mr. Tree-Stump?'" she thought to herself. "And what can you tell me about flying carpets ... and unicorns?"

Perhaps the little creature had left a trail, Rosie thought, very glad that she had learned how to follow tracks at her old school.

She looked out for footprints in the grass and dirt as she walked along. Rosie couldn't see any little tree-stump-creature tracks ... but there were plenty of others. Here and there were marks that looked like hoofprints. They didn't look big enough to have been made by an adult horse, but they could, Rosie thought, belong to a pony or a foal.

Or—and she laughed at how ridiculous a thought this was—could they belong to the unicorn that the little tree stump mentioned?

Rosie didn't mind which it was. Meeting a wild pony would be pretty amazing, too. She followed the tracks along the winding path as it branched off once, and then again. She noticed that she was walking on leaves. Rosie looked up and realized that she was quite deep inside the forest. She had been so focused on her tracking that she hadn't really been paying attention to where she was going. She wasn't worried though—it was a friendly seeming sort of forest. All around her, branches fluttered, and dappled sunlight fell on the soft forest floor.

Whiz! Whizzzzzz! A soft, buzzing hum sounded behind her. Rosie turned around in confusion, expecting to see a bee or wasp.

Whiz! Whizzzzzz! The sound was getting louder. Rosie followed it to a hollow beneath a tall beech tree. Cautiously, she bent down and saw a gleam of silver. She cleared some leaves away and picked the shiny object up. It was a large, heart-shaped pendant, nearly as big as the palm of her hand.

It buzzed again and Rosie tightened her grip to keep hold of it. To her surprise, she felt it spring open. She gazed in wonder. It was a locket, and inside was a crystal.

★ Oona the Unicorn ★

The crystal was the size of a grape, teardrop-shaped, and glowed with a soft white light. It seemed to be hovering in the locket case. Suddenly, it started to spin! It flickered first one way, and then the other, and then stopped, quivering, with its tip pointing into the forest.

Rosie looked in the direction it was pointing and saw a shape moving far away between the trees. She took two paces forward, then another, and another. The crystal seemed to be pulling her along!

The shape far ahead of her moved again. Just then, a small creature bounced onto the path ahead of her. She smiled as she made out its little ears and a fluffy tail.

"Rosie, where are you?" Her father's voice was enough to startle the little bunny, and it hopped away into the shadows.

She turned and ran back up the path, tucking the locket into her pocket as she went.

"So, you've found Starfall. I used to love exploring here," Dad said, his eyes twinkling.

"Will you show me?" Rosie asked, excited to tell him what she had seen.

"Yes, we can go for a long walk when we've unpacked more," he sighed and looked back to the house. The rest of the day was spent unpacking and sorting, but Rosie's mind kept wandering back to the forest and the locket.

Rosie hadn't slept very well. First, because of the noise—it sounded like someone was playing a tuba under her window, which made absolutely no sense at all. Second, because her airbed had gone right down. She couldn't wait to have a proper bed again.

She tucked the pretty silver locket carefully into her pocket as she dressed, before going downstairs. Her parents were at the newly unpacked kitchen table munching on toast. Rosie spent the morning loading books onto the bookcases. It was really boring, and she desperately wanted to go into the forest.

When her mother said she was going into the village after lunch, Rosie agreed to go too. Anything was better than unpacking!

It was a five-minute walk before they started to see a few other wonky old houses appearing. When they reached the village, it was just three stores, a duckpond, and a small playground. Rosie asked if she could play there while her mother ran errands.

"OK, but stay right here," her mother replied. Rosie turned to go in, but stopped. Swinging higher than she thought was possible, was another girl.

Rosie hesitated, suddenly a little bit shy.
The other girl spotted her, waved, and slowed
her swing down.

"It's alright," she called over. "Come and
join me!" She had a great big smile and her
hair was a riot of black curls.

"I'm Kat," she said, as Rosie drew near.
"I already know who you are. You're the new
people at Kooky Cottage. There are no secrets
in Springhaven ... you get a new toothbrush,
everyone knows if it's green or blue! That's
what my Nana says." Rosie laughed.

"Yes, we just moved in. But I guess you know that. I'm Rosie." She sat down on the swing and pushed off the ground. She hadn't been on a swing for ages, and grinned as she instantly remembered how much she loved the feeling of whooshing through the air.

"It's going to be great having someone else my age in the village," said Kat. She had a bubbly way of talking and Rosie was glad to have found a friend. She opened her mouth to ask Kat about the forest and the tree stump, but Kat spoke first.

"You have to tell me all about Kooky Cottage—that's just what I call it—the lady that lived there before was loo-oo-py!" Kat let out a great cackling laugh. "But at least she was different to the other villagers; she used to bring a toad into the café and they all used to squirm! It was so funny!"

"Rosie!" Her mother was calling her from the gate holding a large package. "Come on, let's go!" Rosie got up to leave, but Kat jumped up and followed.

"Oh, can't you stay out longer?" Kat asked, "I'll show you around, I've lived in Springhaven all my life. It will be fun. It's so boring here in the summer!"

"Can I?" Rosie asked her mother. She might have a chance to ask about the tree stump if she spent more time with Kat.

"Alright. I guess unpacking isn't much fun for you. I'll meet you back here at 4 o'clock, how does that sound?" Rosie smiled and nodded, "Yes, please."

There really wasn't much to see or do in Springhaven, but hanging out with Kat was fun. They went into the smallest store and Kat bought some sprinkle puffs.

"My little brothers go crazy for them; it helps if I'm trying to bargain for something," she explained, tucking them into her bag. Rosie bought a simple necklace to put the locket on.

Next, they went to the café for milkshakes. Rosie chose Sweet Peach and Kat had Choc-Cherry. They were almost better than the ones Rosie used to have in the city. She was waiting for the right moment to ask if Kat had ever heard of unicorns living in the forest, but it was hard to bring it up.

Kat told Rosie about her family. She had younger twin brothers, two cats, four hamsters, chickens, and an iguana.

"It's like living in a zoo," she joked. In turn, Rosie told Kat about her old life in the city, and all about her disgusting new toad wallpaper. Kat laughed out loud when Rosie compared the toads' green to baby poop!

"What about Starfall Forest?" Rosie asked Kat. "Do you go inside?"

"Nah," said Kat, "It's kind of an unspoken rule of the village that you don't go in there. I never really thought about why. Have you?" Rosie hesitated.

"Yes," she said. "Just a little way. And look," Rosie took the locket out of her pocket.

"I found it in the woods. It glows and spins." Rosie rushed on excitedly, "It showed me the way into the forest and I thought I saw a strange creature." Kat raised her eyebrows. The crystal was still and silent, just sitting in the case.

"It's very pretty," said Kat, but Rosie could tell she didn't believe there was anything weird going on. Rosie felt embarrassed … now her story sounded silly and made up.

The clock in the café chimed four, Rosie tucked the locket back in her pocket and jumped off her stool. "I have to go," she said. The girls rushed to the park where Rosie's mother was already waiting for her.

"Let's do something tomorrow," said Kat. Rosie smiled. She was glad Kat still wanted to be friends after the locket story had fallen flat.

"Come to ours?" Rosie said, looking at her mother for her permission.

"Yes, that's a great plan," her mother said. "We're a bit more sorted now and I've got some paint for Rosie's room—perhaps you two would like to help us decorate? You can chat while you paint!"

They waved goodbye to Kat and headed home. When they got back, her father was trying to cook dinner on a tiny camp stove because the kitchen oven still hadn't been fitted properly yet. Rosie rushed upstairs. She had felt the locket quivering in her pocket and wanted to look at it as soon as possible. When she opened it, the crystal was spinning incredibly fast!

Rosie stood by the window, watching the crystal moving. At last it slowed almost to a stop, flickering gently, its tip pointing toward the forest. Rosie put the locket on the new necklace, and fastened it around her neck. She tucked it carefully inside the neck of her t-shirt before going back downstairs.

"I'm just going outside for a bit," Rosie called to her parents.

A muffled "OK" came from the kitchen, and she sped out of the back door, pulling the locket out of her t-shirt as she went.

Rosie jumped down the steps and walked toward the forest. As she passed the fountain, she stopped. Lots of small, silver fish were flitting and darting about in the water.

Beneath them, the bottom of the fountain's basin was now free of the coins she had seen yesterday. Rosie turned and looked around her. Had someone been in and taken them?

She was about to go inside and ask her parents if they had bought the fish, when she remembered the coin she had put in her pocket the day before. She pulled it out and lowered her hand carefully into the water. The moment it touched the surface, it turned into a small silver fish and swam quickly away to join its friends. Rosie watched, amazed.

She felt the locket start to quiver more strongly. She opened it and the crystal span its point toward the forest, just as before. She tried twisting the locket around so that it faced back toward the house or the town, but the crystal kept turning around to point to the forest again.

Following the crystal's quivering point, Rosie hurried to the end of the garden. Just as she stepped over the old fence, her foot nudged something squashy. She shuddered, and whatever it was hopped off through the long grass before she could get a good look at it. From somewhere very close by, there came a loud tuba-like honk. Rosie looked around for the source of the noise but there was nothing there!

She looked down to check the locket and, as she did, she noticed the same hoofprints in the grass as the day before. They seemed to go in the same direction that the locket was pointing. As she entered the trees, Rosie felt her shirt catch and pull against something. She looked and found she seemed hooked to something that simply wasn't there! It felt like it might be a rose bush—she could feel soft petals and sharp thorns, but she simply couldn't see it at all.

Hearing a small sound, Rosie looked up.

"Oh my." She breathed quietly. A short way in front of her, peeking between two trees, was a pearly white foal with a shimmering horn on its forehead.

Rosie stood still, not daring to breathe or make a sound. Very slowly, she reached out a hand to the little unicorn. The animal didn't startle but moved a pace closer. It was small. "It must be only a foal," Rosie thought. She could see that it was limping. One of its forelegs was injured and the foal couldn't use it properly.

"Come here!" Rosie called softly to the animal as she made gentle clicking noises with her tongue.

The foal crept a pace closer and so did Rosie. They went on like this, each taking tiny steps until Rosie's outstretched hand brushed gently against the foal's soft nose.

"There, there" whispered Rosie very softly. "What's your name?"

The foal let out a soft whinny, *Ooonahhh*.

"Oona?" Rosie said, "Yes, that's lovely."

The next moment, Rosie heard her parents calling for her to come in. Oona startled and rushed away into the trees. Even limping, she moved quickly. Rosie felt worried, how could she help an injured unicorn?

That night, before she went to bed, Rosie looked out at the forest. There was no sign of Oona, but in the dusky light she thought she could see something glowing just inside the trees. Could it be the rose bush that had snagged her shirt?

Chapter 3
Into the Forest

Rosie raced down the stairs to let Kat in the next morning. "Hey Rosie!" said Kat, bouncing through the open door. "I've always wanted to use that," she said, pointing to the ferret-shaped brass knocker. Rosie laughed and the two girls went into the kitchen.

"Good morning, Kat," said Rosie's mother. "Do you girls fancy helping out with painting Rosie's room? Rosie can show you around while I get things set up, how's that?"

"Great!" said Rosie. Rosie excitedly showed Kat around the old house. She found she felt almost proud of her quirky home. Then they

listened while Rosie's mother explained what they should do for the painting, but as soon as she left, they started chatting again.

After a while, Rosie said tentatively, "I've seen some really strange creatures around the house, and in the garden—near the forest ..."

"Oooh! Like what?" Kat asked. "Tell me!"

"Well," said Rosie, and she told Kat about the fish in the fountain and her meeting with Oona the unicorn. Kat listened, but from the skeptical look on her face, Rosie could tell that Kat didn't believe her.

For a while, Rosie and Kat painted the room in silence. As they painted over the toads, Rosie had a pang of regret—she was actually coming round to liking them!

"The fish were really silvery," Rosie said eventually. "My coin changed as soon as it touched the water."

"Uh huh," said Kat. Rosie painted quietly for a while, then said: "It took me ages to coax Oona close enough to stroke her nose. Her limp is really bad. I wouldn't know who to tell about a hurt unicorn."

"Oh, well, maybe the magical animal welfare brigade can help," Kat sniggered.

Rosie was hurt—it was so unfair of Kat not to believe her, and she didn't know how to convince Kat that she was telling the truth. She took her paint pot across the room and started painting near the window. The girls didn't speak again until Rosie's dad called them down to lunch. Rosie didn't eat much. She so wanted Kat to believe her.

"Wasn't the toad wallpaper awful, Dad?" Rosie said at last.

"I kind of liked it!" her father replied. Kat smiled, but Rosie blinked back hot tears of frustration from her eyes. Why didn't anyone seem to understand how she felt?

"How's the painting going, girls?" Rosie's mother asked.

"It's going well," said Rosie. "We've done lots. Maybe we could take a break, and explore outside for a bit?" She had decided to show Kat the silver fish to prove that she wasn't making it up.

"That's a good plan," said her mother, and when everyone had finished, Rosie led the way outside.

"It's OK, you know," said Kat as they stepped off the back porch. "I like to make stories up too. Yours are really good."

"They aren't stories ... " said Rosie. "Look," she pointed to the fountain and both girls peered into the water. Several bright, silver coins were settled quietly on the bottom of the pool. Rosie stared and stared, willing them to move. She reached into the cool water

and picked out a coin. She turned it over in
her hands, then slipped it back into the water.
It drifted slowly to the bottom and settled.

"Wow! This tree is really cool!" Kat had
wandered off under the big willow tree.

"Back in a sec," said Rosie and walked
into the house. She was going to show Kat
the locket.

Rosie went into her room to find her backpack. She slipped the locket inside and went back into the garden.

"Look!" Kat called from under the tree. She had found an old swing tucked up in the branches and was now getting it going. Rosie's heart sank. Why hadn't *she* found the swing?

Rosie wished as hard as she could for something magical to happen. She wanted Kat to see just how special this place was! Then, the next moment, she felt a tug on one of her shoelaces. She looked down. There, calmly chewing on her shoelace was a toad. This wasn't an ordinary toad, though. For a start, it was at least twice the usual size and its skin was a bright purple, then there were the bright pink horns on its head, and it smelled a bit like cupcakes! Spotted all over its back were small pink spines. It was

obviously really friendly. The toad looked up at Rosie, gave a big grin, and let out a loud *Hooonnnnnkkk!*

Rosie couldn't help giggling. It was so funny looking. She realized, too, that it was the same tuba-like noise that had been keeping her awake at night!

"Kat, come here!" she called, but at the same moment she heard:

"Rosie! Come and look at this!"

At Kat's call, the toad hopped away under the porch. Rosie jumped up and went to see what Kat had found. She was just beyond the tree, looking at something on the ground. Rosie could see she had moved aside some of the long, wild grass and found a flowerbed.

"Listen!" said Kat, turning to her with shining eyes. Rosie crouched quietly beside her. She could hear a faint tinkling sound. Right in front of them was a small cluster of nodding yellow flowers shaped like little bells. Rosie leaned closer—the sound was definitely coming from the flowers. She was about to say something when she heard a familiar buzzing sound.

"Quick!" she said as she darted back to the step. Rosie took the locket from her bag and popped open the case. The crystal was spinning and glowing, just like before. Kat's mouth fell open in surprise.

"It's working! It's working! See?!" Rosie looked up at Kat. For once, Kat was silent, and was just staring at the locket. She opened her mouth to speak but …

Whoooooosh!

Something flew low over their heads and then up and away over the forest. It was big and rectangular and left a trail of rainbow cloud! Rosie could just make out two figures on top. One had a pointed hat, the other what seemed like a long swishing tail!

"It's the flying thing!" called Rosie.

"You've seen it before?" Kat asked.

"Yes, early on the very first morning here!" Rosie squeaked with excitement.

Kat looked at Rosie, and Rosie looked at Kat. Without a word, both girls rushed down the path and over the fence. They

plunged into the trees, only just able to see the rainbow trail in the sky. They ran as fast as their legs would take them, until eventually they had to stop, both panting hard.

"I ... can't ... see ... it ... anymore ... " Rosie huffed.

"Me ... either ... " Kat breathed.

While they recovered, they looked around them. They were deep in the forest. Rosie wondered if perhaps they should go back to the house, but she was sure they wouldn't be out for long. Besides, she might be able to show Kat more of the magic!

"What do you think it was?" Kat asked, excitedly.

"I don't know," Rosie replied, she was hesitant to say what she really thought.

"It looked," Kat said slowly, "like a magic carpet ... "

Rosie had thought so too. "Yes!" she said, "and I thought I saw someone with … "

"… a pointed hat and a long fluffy tail?" Kat finished for her. Rosie nodded. She grinned, and Kat did too.

"I guess there are some pretty strange things around here after all!" Kat said. Rosie was so relieved that Kat was starting to see she hadn't been making anything up. "What now?" Kat asked. There was no sign of a path.

"I know!" said Rosie, taking the locket out of her bag. The crystal started to glow, span gently, and came to rest pointing between two trees. Nervous and excited, the girls followed its direction. Rosie thought it might send them in the direction of the flying carpet, but instead it led them to something else.

"Hey, what's that?" Kat whispered after they had walked a little way. Rosie looked.

Between two trees was funny little creature that looked like a small ball of yellow fluff with arms and legs. The girls crept closer.

The creature was busy picking something from a gnarled, old tree. It had bright pink eyes and tiny little wings. They crept closer still. The fluffy thing was not alone. Twenty or more fluffy balls, in every shade imaginable, fluttered around the gnarled trees, too busy to notice the girls. They were stuffing small baskets with little white objects that were growing on the tree moss.

"Doesn't it look like the trees are growing fluffy marshmallows?" Rosie whispered and Kat nodded.

The next moment there was a sudden, loud squeak and all the fluffball creatures went into a big huddle. As they huddled they seemed to grow brighter, then all at once they broke apart and, as one, rushed out of the clearing.

The fluffy creatures flittered and squeaked from tree to tree before coming to rest by the side of an old oak. They were making such a lot of noise that Rosie and Kat could easily follow the fluffballs without worrying about the creatures hearing them.

The girls stood a little way back as the creatures scampered around the tree before gathering together in a huddle again. Then, they all crowded around a great lump in the bark. With a huge collective effort, they pressed against it and at once the bark fell in and a tiny opening appeared. Each fluffy thing made a little squeak of excitement before diving into the dark gap. Once the last one had jumped in, the tree returned to normal and Kat and Rosie stared at each other in total amazement.

Chapter 4
The Tunnel in the Tree

Kat and Rosie stepped silently out of their hiding place. The trunk of the oak tree was vast, as wide as Rosie's outstretched arms. They found the lump that the creatures had pressed. Rosie ran her hands over it. Was she imagining it, or did it feel warm to the touch? It felt like it was vibrating slightly, a bit like the locket did. "Press it," urged Kat.

Rosie bit her lip, "I don't know," she said. "Anything might happen!" She thought of her parents, who didn't know where she was.

"Go on," said Kat. "Let's try, I want to find out what those little fluffy things were!"

The Tunnel in the Tree

Kat put her hands over Rosie's and they pressed the lump. The bark moved again to show the opening, this time to reveal a spiral wooden staircase. Shaking a little, Rosie stepped inside the tree. She took a few paces down and heard Kat behind her. Thump! The girls turned to look behind them. The tree had closed up again. "Only one way to go now," said Kat, grinning. Rosie felt less sure, but she carried on down the spiral steps into a tunnel flooded with golden light.

The girls could just make out the gaggle of fluffy creatures bobbing along far ahead of them. They walked along the long tunnel, ducking their heads where tree roots hung from the ceiling. Every few steps, little glowing lights were set into the walls. When Rosie stopped to examine one, she saw that it was wiggling and jiggling around. She wondered if it was a firefly or a glowworm.

They had been walking along the tunnel for what seemed like ages when Kat said,

"Hey, they've gone! And what's that?"

They had rounded a corner in the tunnel and, Kat was right, the little cluster of fluffy creatures had vanished. Ahead of them was an old-fashioned bell and a curious set of doors of various sizes.

"Look here," said Kat, and she pointed to sign fixed to the wall:

The Tunnel in the Tree

CALICO COMFREY'S VETERINARY SURGERY

Welcome one, and welcome all,
Magical creatures of Starfall!
Whether dragon, toad, or unicorn,
With injured tooth or paw or horn,
Come inside—this magic's real—
Our team of vets are here to heal!

The girls kneeled beside the smallest door. Rosie opened it, peeped inside, and let out a gasp.

It looked like a scene from a picture book! A strange dragon was asleep on a white pillow-covered bed. It had shimmering jade-blue scales, cute little horns, tiny wings, sharp claws, and a long tail which curled around and rested near its nose. With every outbreath, little puffs of light smoke escaped from its nostrils. Then, it gave a little hiccup

and enormous fiery sparks exploded from its nose, mouth, and ears!

Just then, a face appeared in the medium-sized doorway right in front of them. Rosie and Kat jumped back in alarm. It was a wooden face with a green moss-tache jumping about on its face. It was the tree-stump-creature Rosie had seen bustling about near the shed! "What's this? What's this? What's this? Are you coming in, or aren't you? Don't just stand there, letting the wind in."

With that, the medium door closed, and the tree-stump-creature pulled the big door open and ushered the girls inside. Kat and Rosie took a step but the tree-stump-creature pulled them in, and slammed the door behind them. The tree-stump-creature said, a little imperiously: "Quibble's the name. Surgery porter. What's the trouble?"

Rosie and Kat couldn't believe their eyes. The room was cavernous, and full of noise and commotion. The fluffy creatures they had followed into the tree were everywhere! The dragon opened her eyes, saw the newcomers and gave another great fiery hiccup that filled the room with thick white smoke.

"Now, now, now, that's quite enough of that." Quibble motioned to one of the fluffy creatures who began to flap the smoke away. As the room slowly became clear again, Rosie made out the shape of a great bird sitting on a perch not far away. It was majestic but looked like smoke was gently wafting from some of its bright red feathers.

"It must be a phoenix," Rosie thought. Kat nudged her and nodded to the other side of the room where a truly enormous caterpillar was asleep in a huge pile of the marshmallow flowers that they had seen the little fluffy creatures collecting. Beyond it, in the middle of the room was what looked a little bit like a small badger, but its fur was a patchwork of green squares. The girls stepped back as a fox with three tails sauntered past giving each of them a good sniff as it went. There were more fluffballs everywhere.

"Now then, no time for idling." Quibble was tugging on Rosie's sleeve. "Are you visiting someone?"

"No, well, we, um ... " As Rosie started to speak, a little man rushed in from a door at the other end of the room. He was half the size of Rosie and Kat and was wearing a green, pointed hat with mushrooms growing from it, big, round glasses, and a stethoscope around his neck. He hurried up to the dragon and put his stethoscope to its chest. As he did, the dragon gave a smoky hiccup, and the little man turned around, spluttering.

The Tunnel in
the Tree

When he was able to open his eyes again, he spotted Rosie and Kat.

"Oh my spoons and jars ... Normilliams! In the hospital!" He gaped at them.

"What, what, what?!" squeaked Quibble. "These girls are Normilliams? Oh my worms and wishmice and woodlice! Oh dear, normal people can't be in here! No, no, no! Oh dear, out, out, out you must go!" And he started pushing the girls back out of the door.

Rosie spoke quickly: "Wait, please!" She managed to dodge around Quibble and up to the little man. "Please. We're very worried about a baby unicorn. The sign said magical creatures ... are you a magical vet?" The little man frowned.

"I'm Doctor Morel. Hmm, a foal ... " he murmured, stroking his beard. He turned to Quibble, "Take them to Doctor Clarice."

Frowning, Quibble led the way down a long, earthy corridor. Rosie turned anxiously to Kat who nodded excitedly and followed.

Quibble coughed to announce himself as he held open a glass door for Rosie and Kat. The girls found themselves in a room full of strange gadgets and beeping equipment. One table was filled with fizzing and bubbling glass bottles and tubes. Leaning over a device that seemed to be made of wires and springs, was a

young woman with bright red hair and round glasses. She stood up when they entered.

"Doctor Morel asked me to bring these ... visitors," Quibble huffed, "to you. Something about a unicorn." And with that, he stomped out of the room.

"Well, hello," she said, smiling. "How can I help?"

Rosie was relieved that Doctor Clarice was friendly. "We found you by accident," she said.

"We followed some tiny fluffy things." Kat finished, and Rosie nodded.

"Ah, the flutterpuffs," said Doctor Clarice. "Well, why don't you follow me on my rounds, and tell me as we go." They started back down the corridor, "Don't mind Quibble," she said. "The safety of the animals is our top priority and usually we don't let Normilliams—sorry, normal people—in."

Doctor Clarice led the girls into a cavelike room that was dark and hot. A fire burned in the middle, and set around the edge were large shiny green eggs.

"Rare cloud dragon eggs," she explained. "We're looking after them while we treat the mother for hiccups."

After checking the eggs, Doctor Clarice led Rosie and Kat into a room that looked like a big green field. Dotted here and there were small holes made in the turf.

"Now, about the unicorn ... " she asked, bending over one of the holes and sniffing.

"Yes," said Rosie eagerly and told Doctor Clarice everything that she could remember about her meeting with Oona. "I managed to stroke her but my parents called me just then, which startled her and she ran away. She was limping badly." Rosie finished.

The Tunnel in the Tree

Doctor Clarice looked very worried. "We knew something was wrong. The starflowers are closed, the flutterpuffs are jittery, even the oldest trees are drooping—the whole forest is affected by the unicorns, especially the foals." She sighed and stood up. "It wouldn't be so hard to find her if we could find our crystalzoometer!" Doctor Clarice explained, "At least, that's what I call it. Everyone else calls it the crystal thingy."

"A crystal?" Rosie asked, "Is this it?" She pulled the locket out of her bag and Doctor Clarice smiled with relief.

"You've found it! Oh, thank goodness!" Doctor Clarice clapped her hands and took the locket.

"Right, now, we must get on!" She said, but just at that moment, the large, green badger ambled through the door.

"There you are!" said Doctor Clarice, "Come along, back to your bed." She ushered the badger toward the doorway and turned back to the locket. The badger sniffed the air, and then suddenly all its fur stood straight out on end. Rosie and Kat giggled—Doctor Clarice turned to look.

"Oh no! Run!" She shouted, but it was too late. A great BOOM! exploded from the badger and the room was filled with green clouds that smelled exactly like rotten eggs. Coughing and spluttering, they all covered their mouths and ran for the door.

The Tunnel in
the Tree

"Sorry about that," said Doctor Clarice, fanning her nose, "Boombadgers are not the most fragrant creatures when they're sick. Wait here a second … " and she bustled off.

Rosie and Kat stood in the corridor taking deep breaths of fresh air. When they had recovered, Rosie started looking around, but Kat gave a small sniff. "I really am sorry I didn't believe you, before, I mean, about the unicorn," she was looking at her feet.

"That's OK," said Rosie. "It was pretty unbelievable!" Both girls laughed.

"Best friends?" Kat asked, and Rosie nodded.

"Always!" she said, smiling.

Chapter 5
The Crystalzoometer

"**R**ight," Doctor Clarice joined them moments later, and they set off back down the long corridor again. They followed her up a steep spiral staircase. As they climbed, they noticed windows placed here and there. The view changed from forest floor to tree branches, and then to open sky. At last they stepped out on a platform and Kat gasped. They were at the top of an immensely tall pine tree. There was a rail around the edge and attached to it were all sorts of spyglasses.

"Each of the telescopes shows us something different," Doctor Clarice explained.

Rosie stepped up to the rail. She put one eye up to the end of the nearest spyglass—everything was blue, and split into triangles. Kat stepped forward and looked through one: "It's all upside down!" she said. Kat looked through another that showed them the forest, but everything was a little off. Doctor Clarice said that it showed the forest 1,000 years ago. The next one Rosie looked through showed different-sized, bright red spots moving about. Doctor Clarice explained that each spot was a magical creature—except for the unicorns.

Doctor Clarice walked over to a long, ornate, wooden telescope. She opened the locket and took out the crystal.

"We use this one to look for unicorns," she explained. "Crystals can power lots of magical machinery!" She deftly fitted the crystal into a slot behind the eyepiece, and the telescope soon began to glow and vibrate. She spent a moment scanning the forest, then cried out: "There she is!" Doctor Clarice took a step back from the telescope and let Rosie look. It took a moment for her eyes to adjust. In the diamond-shaped patch of light at the end of the telescope, she could see the forest, but she could see right through the trees, like an x-ray. She scanned the bright white picture then spotted a yellow shape. It was Oona.

"I can see her! Oona! Look!" Kat looked, and gasped at her first sight of the unicorn.

"She's moving … " Kat stood back and let Doctor Clarice look again.

"Oh no," Doctor Clarice said. "I think she's heading for Mazewood. If she goes in any deeper, she could be lost forever!" The doctor removed the crystal and placed it back into the locket. Then, she rushed back to the door in the tree and Kat and Rosie followed.

When they reached the bottom of the spiral staircase, Doctor Clarice led the two girls down a long, twisting corridor to another room. Rosie and Kat stifled squeals of delight, and Doctor Clarice smiled at their reactions.

Right in front of them, floating in mid-air, was a kind of old-fashioned woven carpet.

The type you might find in an old house or museum, it was quite thick and covered with a pretty pattern of green leaves and pink and purple flowers. It rippled gently as it hung in the air.

"I'll just get a tracker," said Doctor Clarice as she took a device down from a shelf. It was about the size of a small book and had a long strap that she hung around her neck, and lots of knobs and buttons.

"Climb on!" She said to the girls, who were still staring in amazement. "This is our ambulance. It was too slow so I've fitted a motor on the back. It runs on bubble liquid." She took a bottle from the shelf, filled a small container on the machine, and pulled a lever. A stream of rainbow bubbles flew from the back of the motor, Doctor Clarice jumped onto the carpet, and they were off!

Kat let out a delighted squeal and Rosie closed her eyes tightly as the magic carpet whooshed forward. It seemed as if they were going to fly straight into the wall! But what they had assumed was a painting of green leaves parted at their approach. They sped out into the forest and up into the air.

"Look!" Kat pointed to some small people who were bustling

around with watering cans. Kat was intrigued, and opened her eyes. Small, wooden doors were set into the trees all around them.

"Ah, gnome homes," said Doctor Clarice, looking down. "Doctor Morel's cousins if I'm not mistaken."

"Do you help look after the sick or injured gnomes and fairies, too?" Kat asked.

"No, we can't," said Doctor Clarice, "that would be like you going to the vet for help! We can only help the magical animals. The gnomes have a gnomitrician. And the fairies have their fairy godmother, of course. She is very clever."

"Now then," suddenly Doctor Clarice was directing the carpet down through a clearing and into a beautiful green glade. The girls had to hang on to each other and to the edge of the carpet to avoid falling off!

"Sorry, it does take a little getting used to," Doctor Clarice said as the two girls tumbled onto the floor. "Now, which way?"

As Rosie and Kat picked themselves up, Doctor Clarice turned on the tracker and pulled up a long aerial. She fitted the power crystal into a dial on the front and it lit up and began to spin.

"This way." Doctor Clarice led the way through some trees. "I'm afraid we are going toward Mazewood. It was planted long ago by some imps. They bewitched the trees and bushes to keep changing places. Once inside, you could get lost in there for years. You must both stay close to me."

Rosie and Kat were only half listening—there was so much to look at! Kat bent down to look at some giant orange mushrooms that jumped up and started dancing playfully

around her feet. Doctor Clarice stopped to stroke one. "Goodbye, little funnygi!" Doctor Clarice, chuckling as they walked on.

"Oh no," Rosie exclaimed, "that bird's nest has fallen down!" The nest seemed to be on the wrong side of the branch.

"Don't worry," said Doctor Clarice. "It's just the nest of a topplebottom bird. They fly, lay eggs, and live upside down. It's something to do with an allergy to gravity."

They walked on and on, Doctor Clarice pointing out tracks and homes of magical creatures the girls had never heard of. Just then, the crystal started spinning like crazy and turned a dark green.

"Oh dear," Doctor Clarice said, shaking the tracker gently. "There must be a pixie around here somewhere, they always make things go a bit haywire. I'll have to take the back off and fit a pixabubble around it." Doctor Clarice kneeled down and began taking something from the back of the machine. It looked like a plastic case.

Rosie and Kat watched her for a while, and then began to look around them in wonder. The forest made all kinds of unusual creaks and whispers. Kat thought she saw a golden-yellow snake disappearing behind a tree, but when they peered around, it seemed to be

an enormously long tail.
They never even saw the
creature it was attached to!
Doctor Clarice was
still fixing the little
machine, which
now had a pair
of headphones
attached to it.

Just then, Rosie
heard a quiet "crack" a
little way away. She span around.
There, between two trees was Oona.
Rosie tiptoed forward, then stopped.

"Go on!" said Kat.

"Shhhh," Rosie said, creeping further still

"Quick!" said Kat but Rosie shushed her
again, she knew how timid Oona was.

"Wait here ... " she whispered.

Rosie moved as quickly and as quietly as she could toward Oona. She didn't realize how fast she was going until she had to catch her breath, and she heard Kat panting behind her. Oona was still ahead of them but she was moving quickly away through the trees.

"Can you try to call her back again?" Kat asked. Rosie made the clicking noise, but Oona went further into the trees.

"We need to help her," she breathed.

"I thought she knew you?" said Kat. She sounded a bit annoyed. Rosie looked up.

"Which way did we come from?" she asked. The two girls turned around to find a thick tangle of trees behind them.

"I don't know," said Kat.

"Well, at least we can try to help Oona," said Rosie. "And I'm sure Doctor Clarice will catch us up." She took a few steps forward.

Kat followed, but tripped over a tree root hidden in the leaves. Hearing her cry, Oona startled and bolted away into the trees.

The two girls stared after her, Kat sprawled on the floor, Rosie still reaching out toward the lame foal. Silence fell around them. The trees whispered, and somewhere high above them, something giggled.

Chapter 6
Lost and Found

"I can't believe you just did that!" Rosie shouted at Kat, who was sitting on a tree stump, looking at her shin.

"Me?!" Kat said looking up. "You were the one that wandered off. And I've hurt my leg in case you hadn't noticed!"

"I said to wait!" Rosie huffed, "If you'd stayed, you could have told Doctor Clarice which way Oona had gone, and she would have helped us to find her."

Kat stood up, dusted herself down, and limped over to sit on a tree stump. Rosie went and sat on another one nearby. An awkward

silence fell between them. Kat's shin was quite painfully grazed, and Rosie felt bad. But she was still a bit annoyed at Kat for frightening the unicorn foal away.

Just then, a log nearby began to wobble and shudder. Squeaking noises were coming from beneath it. Both girls jumped up and saw the log roll away.

There was a hexagonal hole in the ground where the log had been a moment before. Popping up from one of the holes was a set of long, fluffy, black-and-yellow ears and tiny, springy antennae. A fluffy head followed, and then a stripy body and a cottonball tail! This was no ordinary rabbit.

"Wow!" Rosie squealed. Kat grinned at the creature, who was squeaking at them madly. Kat reached out a hand and let

the bunny sniff it, before tickling it behind the ears—the bunny wriggled with delight and started buzzing like a big bee. Then it stopped buzzing and disappeared back inside the hole.

The next moment it was back with a small parcel that it held out to them. Inside the leafy parcel was a sort of cake made of nuts and berries all glued together with ...

"Honey!" The girls said together after tasting a small piece each.

"So, you're a honeybunny?" said Rosie and the bunny nodded proudly.

Roaaaaaaaaaaaaaaaarrrrrrrrrrrrrrrrrrrrrrrrrrrrr!

A tremendous noise shattered the peace in the forest. Rosie and Kat were tumbled aside as the frightened little honeybunny hurriedly disappeared back into its burrow, pulling the log back into place to hide the entrance.

Kat and Rosie stood very close together. They both felt a little bit scared. The woods had gone quite dark and before long the echoing *roaaaarrrrr!* sounded again.

They peered this way and that. Then something fluffy slowly drifted down to land at their feet. It looked like a fluffy seed from a dandelion, but much bigger. Rosie picked it up. A low growl sounded immediately above them. When they looked up, the girls grabbed hold of one another.

On the branch just above their heads, peering down at them, was a majestic lion. Rosie stared. It was strange to be curious and frightened at the same time. The creature in the tree had the face and body of a lion, but around its neck billowed a great white fluffy cloud of seeds. The girls took a few paces backward, and the lion jumped lightly down from its branch. Both girls wanted to run, but they were frozen to the spot. The lion sniffed them, then gave an enormous sneeze, which made his mane of fluff fly from his head and into the air. Through the cloud of seeds falling around them, Rosie and Kat watched in wonder as they saw him shake his head as lots of bright yellow petals sprang up and surrounded his face.

Rosie bravely took a step toward the lion and reached out her hand.

"Please don't eat me!" she whispered, more to herself than the lion. He stepped forward, sniffed her hand and gave it a soft lick. Then, with a growling purr, he rubbed his velvety, flowery head against her body just like an enormous cat. Rosie tickled him behind the ears and admired his glorious yellow petals.

Then the lion stepped back, and gave a small rumbling call, and from every tree, bush, and other hiding place sprang small cubs.

The dandylions, as they later found out they were called, were all bright yellow and had manes of petals around their necks. Lots of adorable little cubs played in the clearing, springing off branches, wrestling with their siblings, and jumping over logs as Rosie and Kat tried to count them—but there were so many that they gave up and watched the cute cubs gambol around.

Then Rosie had an idea. She went up to the biggest dandylion and gently stroked his soft nose.

"Please," she said. "We are looking for an injured, lost unicorn foal called Oona. Have you seen her?" He turned, and for a moment held her gaze with his big amber eyes.

The dandylion called to one of the young ones, and nuzzled his ear gently. The younger dandylion looked over at the girls as if to say, "Follow me," and then set off at once with his nose to the floor. Kat and Rosie followed, waving goodbye as they went.

They followed the small dandylion as he padded silently through the trees on his soft paws. Finally he stopped, beckoned them forward, then turned and moved lightly away. Rosie stepped forward and peered through the trees.

Before her was a beautiful, sunlit glade, and there, drinking from a lilypad, was Oona. She was holding her front foreleg up. Rosie and Kat tiptoed forward. Oona looked up, but she did not run away. The girls moved as softly as they could, one tiny step at a time. When they had gone a little way, they stopped. Kat took something from her pocket and held it out to Oona. It was a bit of the honeybunny's honeycake.

They waited patiently, and soon enough Oona took a step toward them. She came a little closer, and then, after two more steps she was close enough to stretch out her neck and take the honeycake from Kat.

Rosie watched Oona take a little of the honeycake. Her limp was worse than ever now—she could hardly use her front leg. She was also obviously really hungry and tired. "We need to get help as soon as we can," Rosie thought.

Once Oona had taken the honeycake, Kat stroked her soft nose and Oona came closer to them. Rosie stretched out her hand and patted the foal's soft face and neck. Up close, she could see the way that Oona's fur glistened in the light trickling through the trees above.

"She's so beautiful," breathed Kat as she stroked Oona's nose. Her horn was small, and it twisted in a spiral straight up from her forehead. It shimmered like the most perfect pearl. Her long mane glinted in the dappled sunlight as if had been spun from purple gemstones, and she had the most unusual jet-black eyes. The two girls were totally lost for words—they had never seen a creature so utterly lovely.

After a few minutes, Rosie looked at Kat and said, "We're still lost, and we don't know how to make Oona better. How will we ever get her to the surgery?"

Chapter 7
Help for Oona

As Rosie and Kat stroked Oona's head and neck, they began to understand just how exhausted the little foal was. She rested her head against them and wouldn't put her sore leg to the floor at all. Ever so gently, Rosie tried to look at Oona's leg, but she jumped away and skittered back to the other side of the pool.

"Oh no," said Rosie. "Not again."

"It's OK," said Kat. "She knows us now. And we know what she likes!"

"But she's eaten all of the honeycake," said Rosie.

"Yes, but I have these!" Kat took her bag from her shoulder and pulled out a bright package. It was the sprinkle puffs she had bought in the village. She poured some into her hand and held them out to Oona.

Oona sniffed the air, and limped toward the brightly frosted treats. Soon she was close enough to take a little nibble and she nodded and whinnied with delight.

"How are we going to get her back to Doctor Clarice?" Rosie wondered aloud. They stared at the trees with their gently swaying branches. To their great surprise, in the next moment, a great beech tree seemed to shift and lift itself out of the ground. With a great twisting motion, it turned around, shuffled and re-rooted itself. The way they had come was completely unrecognizable.

"Well, we know roughly which direction to go in … " Kat started, but she didn't sound particularly hopeful.

Just then, Rosie felt a gentle nudge behind her. She turned to see Oona's head pushing her shoulder. "We don't know where we're going." Rosie spoke very softly, and Oona nudged her again and stepped forward. Then she turned back and used her nose to gently nudge Kat forward too.

"I suppose she knows best?" Kat said. Rosie nodded and started walking.

Every now and then, Oona raised her head up and seemed to look up into the trees. Rosie looked up too.

"There!" she said, after a little while, pointing up to where a silver ribbon seemed to be trailing across some low leaves. It looked like the prettiest spider's web ever.

"Do you think that's what she's following?" Kat asked.

"Yes, I do," said Rosie.

It seemed that they were right. Oona kept following the winding path of the silver ribbon as it stretched from tree to tree through the beautiful, calm forest.

"I wonder what is making it?" Rosie said.

"Do you think she left it here earlier?" Kat asked.

"I don't think so, if the trees keep moving." Rosie said, then gave a sudden gasp that made them all stop. A large green boombadger had wandered out from behind a big tree and was blocking the path. The girls stopped still and covered their mouths and noses. This time though, they were lucky. After giving them a good look, it carried on its way through the woods.

In spite of their worry for Oona, it was hard not to be delighted with the forest. Peeking into a sunny glade, they saw five

curious creatures tumbling about in the sunshine. They had furry bear-like bodies and spotted red-and-black coats that they curled up in as they rolled about!

Oona led Rosie and Kat across a trickling stream where huge, silver fish were gliding through the clear, cool water. They looked up to see a topplebottom bird flying upside down—just as Doctor Clarice had described.

At last they came to a part of the wood where the trees seemed more spaced out and the light was brighter.

"I think we're out of the Mazewood now," said Rosie softly.

"Look!" said Kat, pointing to a nearby tree where the silver ribbon stopped. Oona had her nose close to a branch where a large, pretty silver butterfly was opening and closing its wings in the sunshine.

"So that's what made the trail for us to follow!" Rosie exclaimed. "That's so helpful, thank you! I wonder where we are now."

Thankfully, she didn't need to wonder for long. The very next moment there was a great flurry of squeaking and both girls found themselves surrounded by a cloud of bright flutterpuffs! Pushing her way through them was Doctor Clarice.

"Oh! Thank goodness we've found you at last!" said Doctor Clarice. "I've had half the forest out looking for you."

She clapped her hands together and made a funny clicking noise with her throat, and all the flutterpuffs suddenly disappeared up the nearest tree. Then Doctor Clarice very calmly approached Oona, gently stroked her silky neck, and looked down at her leg.

"And we are so glad to have found you, Oona. We've been very worried!"

Rosie and Kat looked at each other, suddenly nervous. Would Doctor Clarice be angry with them?

"I'm sorry," Rosie spoke up. "I saw Oona and thought I might be able to get to her. It was my fault we got lost."

"No," said Kat. "I followed, and we went together." Both girls hung their heads.

"Don't worry," said Doctor Clarice, kindly. "I know how exciting a first trip to the forest can be. When I was young, I followed some

bugbear cubs that were chasing a flutterpuff. Luckily, Doctor Morel found me and taught me about the forest. I think the forest just calls to some people." She looked dreamily around her, and sighed a happy sigh.

"Bugbears?" Kat asked. "Are they the little spotty bears? We saw some!"

"And Oona followed a butterfly out of Mazewood, it was so pretty … " She looked around but the butterfly and the ribbon were gone.

"Yes, you saw bugbears and a flutterby," said Doctor Clarice. "That's very interesting. Flutterbys are often quite mischievous, but even the trickiest creature will help a unicorn. Luckily, there was a big nest of flutterpuffs just near where you left me. I asked them to help me look for you. The flutterby must have heard too."

"Now," Doctor Clarice said, "Oona, may I examine your leg?"

This time, with Rosie holding her head, and Kat feeding her a few more sprinkle puffs, Oona allowed Doctor Clarice to look at her sore leg.

"She does have a scratch, but it doesn't look very serious." Doctor Clarice took a pot of ointment from her pocket and spread some on the scratch. Then wrapped it neatly in a bandage.

"Does that help?" she said to Oona, but the little foal still would not put her foot to the ground.

"How strange," said Doctor Clarice, taking hold of Oona's hoof. "I can't see anything wrong with it."

Oona began to struggle free and Doctor Clarice let her hoof go.

"I think we had better take you back to the surgery to have a proper look." Doctor Clarice took a small silver whistle from her coat pocket and blew three times. In just a few moments, the magic carpet whooshed into view and hovered, rippling gently beside them at knee height.

"Here," said Doctor Clarice, pushing the carpet down to ground level and spreading out a light silken blanket. Then, with Rosie and Kat's encouragement, Oona climbed on board and they soared up into the sky.

Chapter 8
A Spot of Moonlight

The journey to the veterinary surgery took just a few minutes on the magical carpet. Rosie and Kat thought the ride was better than any roller coaster they'd ever been on! They whooshed and swished through the treetops and soon found themselves back at the surgery. Rosie copied Doctor Clarice's clicking noises to coax Oona off the carpet and they followed Doctor Clarice down the corridor. She took them into a room set out like a horse's stable. Tied to the wall just ahead was what appeared to be a giant sugar cube. Oona ran to it and took a few licks.

With Oona busy at her sugar cube, Doctor Clarice was able to pick up the unicorn's hoof and examine it with a special magnifying glass. The soft part of the hoof looked sore.

"It's very strange," said Doctor Clarice. "It looks like there should be something there, but I can't see anything at all." She bustled out of the room and returned moments later with a strange-looking instrument.

"This is a magnetoscope," she explained, strapping part of the instrument around Oona's hoof. "It's a bit like the x-ray machines in human hospitals." Her head disappeared inside an enormous bubble-shaped helmet. A few moments later her voice echoed from the inside: "Nope. Nothing at all."

Doctor Clarice reappeared and removed the magnetoscope from herself and Oona.

"Well, I think the best thing is to bind it up. Perhaps whatever it was has come out already." She took some balm from a shelf nearby and tried to spread some on Oona's hoof. But the little foal pulled and pulled at her foot whenever Doctor Clarice tried to touch the sore part.

"Oh dear, Oona," said Doctor Clarice. "Where can you have been, I wonder?"

This made Rosie think. "She was near my house," she said. "Perhaps it's a rose thorn?"

"But we'd be able to see that!" said Kat.

"But," said Rosie cautiously, "what about the rosebush near my house that you can't always see? The one that's invisible? My shirt snagged on it the first time I came into the forest. I could feel it, but I couldn't see it."

Doctor Clarice jumped up, switched off the light, and rushed out of the room!

Oona stamped her foot. Standing in the dark with a wild animal, even one so sweet as a unicorn foal, was a little alarming. The girls moved closer to each other, waiting to see what would happen. A few minutes later, a pale beam of soft light shone through the door, followed by Doctor Clarice.

"A moonlight lantern," she explained, "the bush is a night rose."

The light fell on the hoof, and all three gasped. A shimmery silver thorn was stuck in the soft part of Oona's hoof. With Kat gently patting her neck, Oona stood still. She seemed to know that something was about to happen.

Doctor Clarice took tweezers from her pocket and as gently as she could, pulled the thorn from Oona's hoof. She took the balm from her pocket, spread some on the

sore spot, and bandaged it gently. Oona tried experimentally to put her injured hoof on the ground, and when she found it better, whinnied with relief.

The girls were very relieved that Oona seemed to be so much better so quickly, and spent a fun half-hour petting her delightedly.

"Hullo, hullo," a voice came from outside the door. "I know that sound!"

The door opened and an old lady came in. She had a sunhat with wildflowers poked into it here and there, a walking stick with more flowers on it, and great big glasses. Her face was round and friendly.

"Hey, Kooky!" Kat said before she could stop herself, then immediately covered her

mouth with her hands and turned bright pink! The witch's round face crinkled into a smile that showed a bright gold tooth.

"Yes, I thought I heard some Normilliams were here." She smiled. "Rather than using my village nickname, I'll introduce myself properly. My name is Doctor Hart."

Doctor Hart looked up at Doctor Clarice through crinkled eyes, "Behaving, are we?" she asked.

"Oh yes," said Doctor Clarice. "Rosie and Kat managed to find a unicorn foal deep in Mazewood, and Rosie worked out that she had a thorn from a midnight rose stuck in her hoof."

"Goodness," said Doctor Hart. "Not many people could coax a unicorn, especially a foal. Or find their way out of Mazewood!"

Kat and Rosie beamed with pride.

"I expect Oona tried to visit me," Doctor Hart said, and stroked Oona's soft nose. "I used to live at Willow Cottage and I looked after Oona's mother when she gave birth. I tried to explain that I was moving but I'm not sure a unicorn can understand something like moving to a new house."

"I live in Willow Cottage now," Rosie said.

"Ah, well I am very glad someone young is living there. I loved the old place dearly, but it made more sense for me to live at the surgery. My father's old treehouse was still here, you see ... "

Rosie and Kat looked curious. "Yes, my father lived here and his father, too. My grandfather was Calico Comfrey. You saw his name by the door? He started the surgery when it became too dangerous for magical creatures to wander openly around ... "

"He was quite magical! Old magic that has disappeared now. He found Starfall Forest and called many magical creatures here to protect them. He put spells on the boundaries to keep Normilliams away ... did you ever notice there are no paths into the forest? And, when adults reach the forest edge, they suddenly think of something else, and decide to go another way!" Doctor Hart giggled. "Have you met the groaks yet?"

"Groaks?" Rosie asked. Doctor Hart nodded, smiling.

"Funny, toad-like, horned creatures? They are very jolly but will eat anything and they do like to sing into the night!"

"Oh," said Rosie, "is that what they were?"

Doctor Hart chuckled. "I had a feeling they would creep back in when I moved out. They are don't like cornflakes at all though, so sprinkle some around the garden fence and they will keep away!"

"What about the fountain?" Rosie asked eagerly.

"The fountain?" Doctor Hart asked.

"Yes," said Rosie. "Do you know what makes the fish swim?"

"Aren't they always swimming?" Doctor Hart asked, looking puzzled.

"No," said Kat. "Sometimes they are silver coins, and sometimes they turn into beautiful silver fish."

"Goodness," said Doctor Hart, "I never knew that. My father put it there. Perhaps," she said with a twinkle in her eye, "the fish only swim when the secret of their magic is safe? They must have trusted you, Rosie."

"Now," said Doctor Hart, "time is ticking along. Perhaps you two had better go home?" Rosie and Kat were disappointed.

"Unless," said Doctor Hart, "you'd like to help with a few more patients?"

"Oh yes, please," Rosie and Kat said together.

Chapter 9
Calico Comfrey's Veterinary Surgery

Kat and Rosie had the most wonderful afternoon helping the magical vets. First, Rosie helped Doctor Hart to bandage a firkin with a broken branch. The firkin was tall and skinny and looked almost exactly like a small pine tree, except that she had twinkling green eyes halfway up her trunk.

Kat's first task was to bathe a bubble-runner—a creature about the size of a mole, but bright blue. It had slipped and fallen into a puddle of sap from a firkin and its fur was so stuck together that it couldn't move.

She was delighted when, after it was washed and dried, the bubblerunner blew a great bubble from his nose and rushed away inside it, exactly like a hamster in a ball!

Rosie was delighted to help an anxious collywobble—it had soft fur, and a long, feathered tail—her treatment was a simple hug! Doctor Hart said that she visited most days for cuddles. Rosie was just admiring the collywobble's glorious tail feathers when Doctor Morel came in: "Look," he said, showing them a ball of fluff. He ran a finger along its back and its fur became shiny green scales! He ran his finger along it once more. Each scale became fluffy again. "A rare snicksnack!" he said excitedly.

"Rosie! Kat! Come here and see!" Doctor Clarice's voice echoed through the twilight room where Rosie was watching Kat feed a pair of baby dingbats. They weren't so much bats as tiny little bells that tinkled sweetly as they hung from a branch near the ceiling.

They followed Doctor Clarice into the cave room. She pointed toward the fire and the girls watched in wonder as one of the eggs wobbled, then cracked and split right open. The mother dragon blew a fluffy cloud from her nostrils that folded like a blanket around the baby who curled up and went to sleep.

Doctor Hart led them back into the main room. "I'm afraid it really is time for you to go home now. It's late in the afternoon and we don't want a search party called!"

"But," Doctor Clarice said, seeing the girls' downcast faces, "we have all agreed that you

can come back at any time. You certainly
both have a touch of magic about you, and
the animals seem to like you, too!"

The girls beamed. Doctor Clarice held out
to them each a shiny silver card. Rosie read
the inscription:

Rosie Fairtree
TRAINEE MAGICAL VETERINARIAN

"Don't worry," said Doctor Clarice, seeing
their worried expressions, "to anyone else's
eyes, they will just look like library cards."

"Oona will show you the way back through the woods," Doctor Hart explained.

Harrumph! came a noise from the corner of the room where little Quibble was busying about with a dustpan and brush.

"It would usually be Quibble's duty," she whispered, "but Oona seemed very keen and we thought it might help her to understand that you live at the cottage now." The girls nodded. Rosie was secretly very glad to have some more time with Oona.

Oona led them along the winding corridor, past the magic carpet take-off room, through the twilight room, and before they knew it the floor beneath their feet had turned to leafy mulch, and they were walking through a low canopy of fuzzy bushes. A little way away, they saw the firkin striding through the trees and wriggling her root-like feet back into the earth. They tiptoed past a huddle of sleeping flutterpuffs at the bottom of a tree.

All too soon, they reached Rosie's garden at the edge of the woods. Kat stroked Oona's neck and Rosie stroked her soft nose.

"See you very soon," Rosie whispered, and Oona gave a soft whinny. Then they stepped out of the woods into the bright sunshine.

They walked in a happy silence to Rosie's gate, then Kat said, "See you tomorrow?"

"Definitely!" Rosie replied, grinning. "See you tomorrow."

That night, Rosie crept out of bed and looked out of the window. The stars twinkled brightly over Starfall Forest. It was beautiful. What a difference a few days could make! Rosie loved her new home. Just then a bright arc of rainbow lit up the sky! The magical vets were off to help another creature. What amazing people, she thought. She was already looking forward to her next adventure.